Ling Cho
and His Three Friends

V. J. PACILIO   Pictures by SCOTT COOK

Farrar Straus Giroux • New York

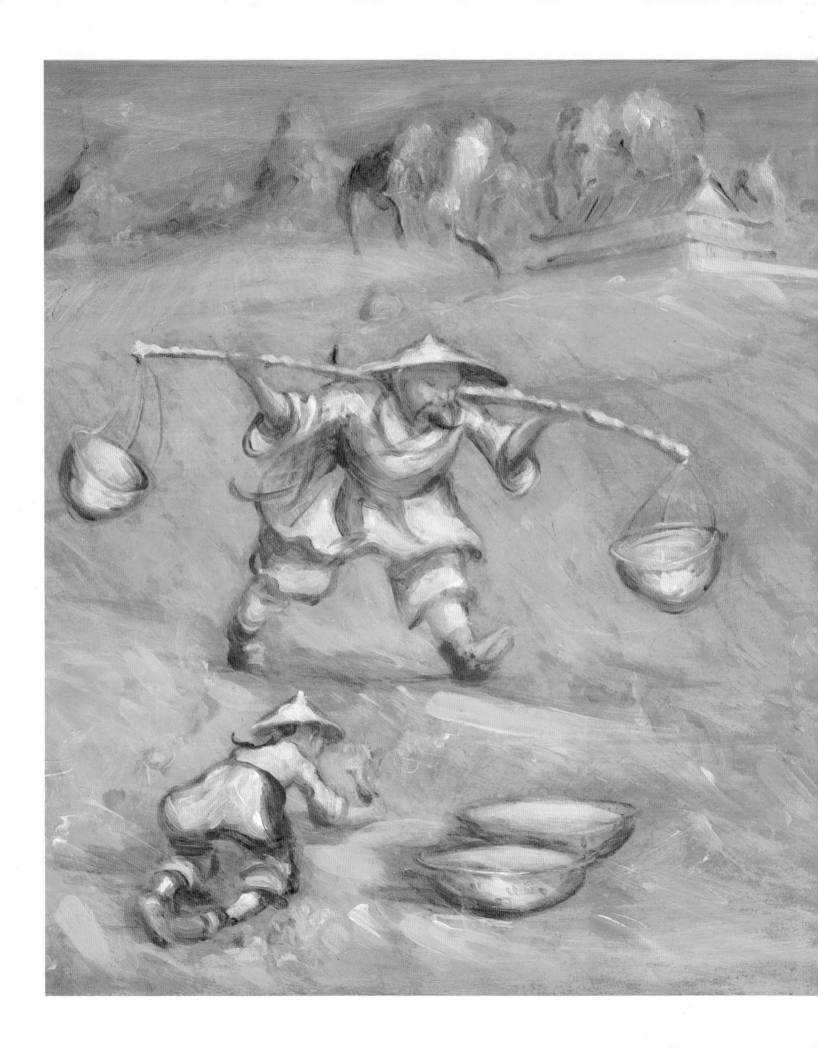

In the wondrous land of China, many years ago,
There lived a wise and kindly man, a farmer named Ling Cho.
Together with his wife and sons, in fertile fields he'd toil;
Their lives entrusted to the land, true servants of the soil.

Each year they plowed, then planted seeds in finely furrowed rows
That stretched in lines as straight as arrows shot from archers' bows.
And when, at last, this grueling task of springtime was complete,
Their crop lay at the mercy of the summer rain and heat.
Arrival of the autumn's harvest moon would then demand
That they summon their resources to the task that was at hand.
With sickles slashing steadily through tawny stalks of wheat,
They'd reap from dawn till dusk, until the harvest was complete.

When once more the moon grew full, a feast they'd then prepare.
As a gesture of thanksgiving, with their neighbors they would share
All the fruits of their good fortune, all that fate had sent their way;
With food and wine and merriment enough to last the day.

From the west would come their friend Ben Lo; Tsung Tae came from the east;
While from the north Quan Jen came forth to join the yearly feast.
With wives and children each would come before the sun did rise;
They celebrated through the night, and then said their goodbyes.

As Ling Cho watched his guests depart this annual affair,
A certain sense of sadness always lingered with him there.
These friends, he knew, would not complain, yet it was plain to see
That none of them had ever been as fortunate as he.
They, too, were born to farming—faithful servants of the land—
But the soil that each inherited was mixed with clay and sand.
Although they worked long hours plowing fields and planting seeds,
The meager crops they did produce did not fulfill their needs.
Now, such was his concern for them that each year Ling Cho tried
To find a way to help his friends that would not hurt their pride.
An outright gift of charity he knew each would reject.
They'd sooner live in poverty than lose their self-respect.

Then one year, as fate would have it, Ling Cho's fervent quest
Would find its resolution as his fertile fields were blessed
With a crop of wheat much greater than he'd ever known before.
The harvest stuffed his storage bins, and still there was much more.
He knew that at the marketplace this surplus could be sold,
So he filled three ox-drawn wagons with as much as they would hold.
He sent his three sons scurrying—one north, one east, one west—
To summon his three neighbors, their assistance to request.

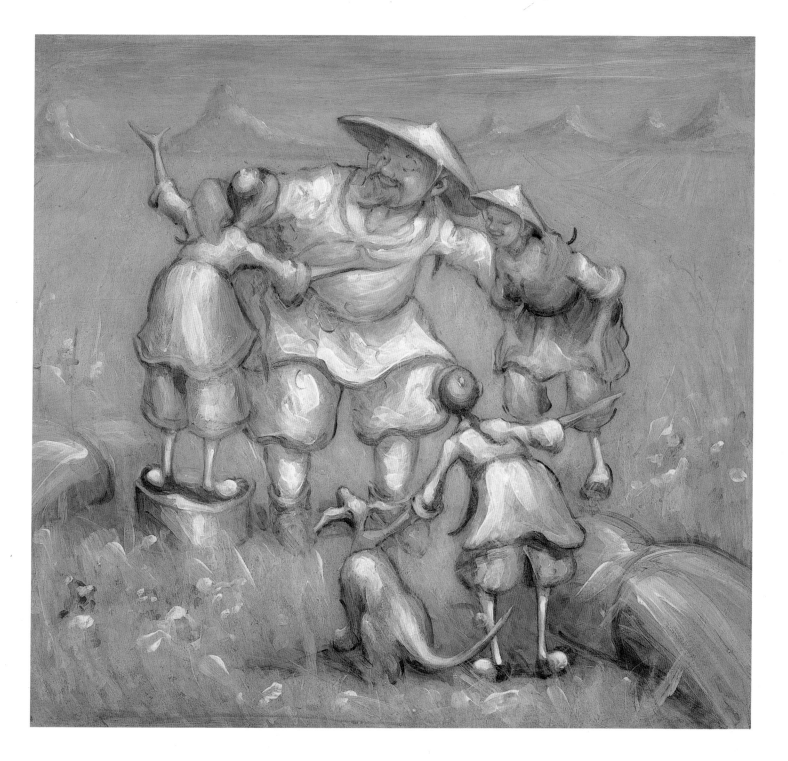

As each arrived, Ling Cho revealed his problem and his plan:
"I've too much wheat to store and I must sell some if I can.
If you'll transport one wagonload to marketplace for me,
When you return with coins of gold, we'll share them equally."
Now, as he had expected, they were eager to comply
As each envisioned all the things those golden coins might buy.

Ling Cho was pleased he'd found a way to help his friends in need,
Knowing they'd be better off because of his good deed.
One by one they then departed. First Ben Lo set out, and then
Next Tsung Tae began his journey, followed lastly by Quan Jen.
For the marketplace they started with their loads of wheat to sell—
Each one destined to return with quite a different tale to tell.

When once again the moon grew full and autumn's winds grew cold,
Ling Cho's three friends returned to feast and share their coins of gold.
The food was on the table when his guests arrived that day,
And all four families celebrated in their usual way.
But when the time, at last, arrived to pay their host his due,
Each offered up a tale of woe and swore it to be true.

"My dear Ling Cho," began Ben Lo, "you'll not like what I say,
But I'm afraid I have no golden coins for you today.
For something dreadful happened on my way to sell your wheat;
A horrible experience I shudder to repeat.
As I approached the marketplace, there came a thunderous roar,
More frightening than any sound I'd ever heard before.
I turned around and found the most outrageous-looking beast
Descending from the hills above, preparing for a feast—

"Instinctively I turned around, intending to retrace
Every step I'd taken since I left the marketplace.
But the light of day had passed away and night had cast its pall.
It became so dark I barely could see anything at all.
So my search was discontinued shortly after it began.
To resume it bright and early in the morning was my plan.
But when daylight came around I found that, much to my dismay,
Rain had fallen through the night and washed the path away.
And though I groped on hands and knees along the muddied ground,
I'm sad to say your two lost coins were nowhere to be found.

"Through pastures filled with clover and lush meadows laced with flowers,
Over hills and through the valleys, till the waning daylight hours
Brought surroundings more familiar to my travel-weary eyes.
And as I turned the path toward home, I came to realize
That the jingling and the jangling were much softer than before.
I thrust my hand inside my vest, its contents to explore.
Were my two coins still there, or were they nowhere to be found?
My fears at once subsided when I heard their jingling sound.
Now my frantic search was shifted to the pocket of my coat
As a lump of apprehension started building in my throat.
It was then that I discovered what I'd hoped would not be true:
Instead of gold, I found the hole your coins had fallen through.

Replied Tsung Tae, "I'm sad to say I cannot pay my due.
Although I sold your wheat for gold, I have no coins for you.
For something dreadful happened and it pains me to admit
I've no one but myself to blame, and that's the truth of it.
As I began my journey home from marketplace that day,
The four gold coins I had received were safely put away.
The shiny pair that were my share were tucked inside my vest,
While the pocket of my coat was where your coins were set to rest.
They jingled and they jangled as my homeward trek began.
Their sound became my cadence as beside the ox I ran

"And so, my friend, it happens that I have no coins today.
I beg your kind forgiveness for this debt I cannot pay.
Perhaps next year at harvest time my help, again, you'll ask.
Then, without doubt, I'll prove that I am equal to the task."

As Ben Lo's story ended, all eyes shifted to Ling Cho
In hushed anticipation of his answer to Ben Lo.
But not one word was said. Ling Cho instead addressed Tsung Tae.
"Have you," he asked, "the golden coins you were to bring today?"

"Again there came that frightful roar; it sent chills down my back.

He pawed the ground beneath him as he readied his attack.

Then with one tremendous leap he landed at my side.

I knew at once his appetite was not to be denied,

So I quickly ducked beneath his grasp and toward the fields I fled.

To my surprise, he spared the ox and ate the wheat instead.

He gnawed and crunched and chomped and chewed and savored every bite.

Then, as quickly as he'd come, he disappeared from sight.

He left me there with nothing but the memory of his face,

And not one single grain of wheat to take to marketplace.

"A creature unlike anything that I had ever seen.
His tail and head were mostly red; his body, shades of green.
Upon his back there grew a stack of sharpened, spike-like things,
And, though he looked too fat to fly, he had a pair of wings.
His eyes were like two burning coals, his ears like moldy bread,
And two black horns, bedecked with thorns, protruded from his head.
His legs were like the trunks of trees entwined with clinging moss.
He stood at least three oxen high and half as wide across.
His nostrils twisted upward as they billowed smoke and ash.
His jaw began to tremble. Then his teeth began to gnash.

"And so, my friend of many years, I come to you in shame,
With no gold coins to give to you and just myself to blame.
Perhaps next year at harvest time my help, again, you'll ask.
Then you will see I, too, will prove I'm equal to the task."

The room grew silent now as Tsung Tae's story reached its end.
Hands folded in his lap, Ling Cho then nodded to his friend.
Now he slowly turned his gaze and nodded once again.
"What tale have you to offer?" he inquired of Quan Jen.
"My dear Ling Cho," began Quan Jen, "I, too, must sadly say
That I have not one single golden coin for you today.
I have no tale of scary beasts, no tale of loss to share;
But rather one of hopelessness, of hunger and despair.

"For fate has not been very kind for many years, you see.
There rarely has been food enough to feed my family.
My children all were sickly and my wife had grown quite weak.
Our future, it was plain to see, was looking rather bleak.
Then one day there came my way the answer to a prayer—
A wagonload of golden wheat to conquer our despair.
And though it was for market meant, I kept your wheat instead.
I ground some into flour and I made it into bread.

"I fed it to my children and I fed it to my wife,
And very soon the sounds of joy came back into my life.
Now my children play once more, my wife is fit and strong.
And though I know, my friend Ling Cho, to keep your wheat was wrong,
Our tomorrows seem more hopeful and the future holds no fear,
For we've food enough in storage now to last us through the year.

"And so, instead of coins for you, my pledge to you I give
That I'll be ever grateful for as long as I may live.
When planting time arrives next year, right by your side I'll stand.
Then I'll return at harvest time to lend a helping hand.
And so shall it continue till my debt has been repaid,
When you decide I've satisfied the bargain that we made.
Whatever you may wish of me, you've only but to ask,
And you will see, I always will be equal to the task."

An air of quiet contemplation settled in the room,
As all three tales had now been told that autumn afternoon.

Evening shadows had appeared before the silence broke.
Now turning to Ben Lo, Ling Cho nodded, then he spoke.

"My dear old friend," Ling Cho began, "your story makes me sad.
I feel somewhat responsible for this ordeal you've had.
For if I had not given you the wheat you were to sell,
You would not have this horrifying, dreadful tale to tell.
'Tis I who should apologize to you—not you to me—
For causing you so much distress and so much misery.
I'm just relieved that you are still alive and well, my friend.
And rest assured, you have my word, this won't occur again.
For I shall not request your help at harvest time next year.
I'm too afraid that frightful beast might choose to reappear.
To tempt your fate in such a way would surely be unwise,
And I'll not be a party to your premature demise."

Turning slightly, Ling Cho now addressed his friend Tsung Tae.
He spoke in softly soothing tones that mirrored his dismay.

"My friend," said he, "it saddens me to watch you in your shame
When I, in fact, myself must share a portion of the blame.
For if you had not sold my wheat at marketplace that day,
No golden coins would you have had to lose along the way.
That mine, and not your own, were lost has caused you guilt, no doubt.
But had your own been in your coat, you'd be the one without.
'Twas fate that did determine what transpired that day, my friend.
And rest assured, you have my word, it won't occur again.
For I shall not request your help at harvest time next year.
That fate, once more, might be unkind is truly what I fear.
Your friendship means much more to me than any coins of gold,
And I'll not chance that guilt and shame might turn that friendship cold."

There now remained to be resolved the fate of only one,
As in the sky the autumn moon had long replaced the sun.
Ling Cho paused for a moment. Then he turned to face Quan Jen.
His voice was cold and harsh as he began to speak again.

"It angers me, my friend," said he, "to hear this tale you tell
To justify what you have done with wheat you were to sell.
To marketplace you were to go, but home you went instead.
You kept my wagonload of wheat and made it into bread.
You speak of sickly children and a wife grown frail and weak,
Of hunger and of hopelessness, a future grim and bleak.
Yet, through these many years of need, until this very day,
Not once did you allow your friends to help in any way.
You let your wife and children share the burden of your pride,
Rather than requesting help that I could well provide.
Then, in desperation, you betrayed me in the end
By taking wheat I gladly would have given you, my friend.

"Now you say that you will stay forever in my debt.
Well, rest assured, you have my word, this pledge I'll not forget.
You'll help me plant my fields each spring, help harvest them each fall.
Throughout the long hot summer, you will answer to my call.
Then, my friend, when all your tasks are finally complete,
You shall receive, as just reward, two wagonloads of wheat.
The first for your consumption, to ensure your family's health,
For therein lies the most important measure of your wealth.
The second, sell at marketplace—the coins you will have earned.
And, I hope, when all is done, this lesson you'll have learned:
A man who will allow his friends to help in time of need
Is—more than even he who gives—a valued friend, indeed."

Four men sat in silence now, with nothing more to say,
Each aware his life was changed by what transpired that day.
And here we take our leave of them, so consequently ends
The story of a wise, kind man, Ling Cho, and his three friends.

For Ferne, Joey, and Eli, my three best friends
—V. J. P.

For Nick
—S.C.

With much appreciation to my editor, Robbie Mayes, and designer, Judy Lanfredi—S.C.

Text copyright © 2000 by V. J. Pacilio
Pictures copyright © 2000 by Scott Cook
All rights reserved
Distributed in Canada by Douglas & McIntyre Ltd.
Color separations by Hong Kong Scanner Arts
Printed and bound in the United States of America by Berryville Graphics
First edition, 2000

Library of Congress Cataloging-in-Publication Data

Pacilio, V. J.
     Ling Cho and his three friends / V. J. Pacilio ; pictures by Scott Cook. — 1st ed.
          p.   cm.
     Summary: Through his plan to share the wealth of his wheat crop with three friends, a
Chinese farmer teaches the importance of allowing other people to help in time of need.
     ISBN 0-374-34545-7
     [1. Sharing—Fiction. 2. Friendship—Fiction. 3. China—Fiction. 4. Stories in rhyme.]
I. Cook, Scott, ill. II. Title.
PZ8.3.P1195Li   2000
[Fic]—dc21   97-50210